Incognito Mosquito Takes To the Air

"This guy is no chop phooey!"

—*Kung Flea*

"We're jist itchin' to have you read this here book!"   —*The Dukes of Buzz-ard*

"Quite a lice book. Rather larvalous, actually."

—*Remington Stole*

Incognito Mosquito Takes To the Air

by E. A. Hass

illustrated by Don Madden

RANDOM HOUSE 🏠 NEW YORK

To Jenny Fanelli
A #1 bug in my book

Text copyright © 1986 by E. A. Hass.
Illustrations copyright © 1986 by Random House, Inc.
All rights reserved under International and Pan-American Copyright Conventions.
Published in the United States by Random House, Inc., New York, and
simultaneously in Canada by Random House of Canada Limited, Toronto.

Library of Congress Cataloging in Publication Data:
Hass, E. A.
  Incognito Mosquito takes to the air.
  SUMMARY: While appearing on a TV talk show, the famous insect detective
describes his adventures outwitting malefactors and solves a mystery on the air.
  1. Children's stories, American. [1. Mosquitoes—Fiction. 2. Insects—
Fiction. 3. Mystery and detective stories] I. Madden, Don, ill. II. Title.
PZ7.H1125In 1986   [Fic]   85-2240
ISBN: 0-394-87054-9 (pbk); 0-394-97054-3 (lib. bdg.)

Manufactured in the United States of America
1 2 3 4 5 6 7 8 9 0

Contents

12:30 A.M. ★ **Channel 13½.**

LATE FLIGHT WITH DAVID LITTERBUG.
Tonight's guests include world-famous detective Incognito Mosquito, who will tell David how he stumbled, fumbled, mumbled, and bumbled onto thrilling solutions for spectacular crimes that confounded other experts.

The following program has been found to contain language that more mature audiences may not understand. Parental desperation is advised.

The material has been carefully screened to keep out undesirable elements. Unfortunately, there are still some bugs in the system. Incognito Mosquito, Private Insective, for one. Not to mention his slippery opponents. You will meet insects so twisted that they have to screw themselves out of bed every morning. You will run into flies so sly that every time they shake your hand, they pump money out of your pocket. You will hear of gnats so gnotorious that they would gnock off their own grandmothers and gnot think a thing of it. And those are the nice guys . . .

Well, he'd finally done it. Incognito Mosquito, Private Insective, had hit the big time. Believe it or not, he was going to appear on the TV talk show *Late Flight with David Litterbug*. That just goes to show what the right kind of press will get you. Hopefully the Mosquito wouldn't get caught in a squeeze play. David Litterbug was a pretty quick wit, and in a battle of wits Incognito Mosquito was completely unarmed.

I.M. was picked up for the show in a Mercedes-Benz stretch limo. And a good thing it did too, or it might have broken

going around those sharp corners. When he arrived at the studio, the Insective was immediately ushered into the Green Room, the place where the guests wait until they go on. The room matched the Mosquito's complexion perfectly. A mosquito with stage fright is not a pretty sight. I.M. was really tied up in knots. Luckily, he managed to unwind before show time.

As the show's opening music played, David Litterbug strolled on stage. He looked calm and cool, as though nothing could shake him. However, he had yet to meet Incognito Mosquito, Private Insective.

David gave the Mosquito a great build-up, introducing him as "the Tick Tracy of the insect world." But as Incognito came onstage, Litterbug's smile turned to a look of sheer confusion. The famed insective had a brown paper bag over his entire head. Only his antennae and nose stuck out. And his nose did stick out.

"Did *our* makeup department do that to you, Mr. Mosquito?" Litterbug asked as the audience roared.

Incognito Mosquito shook David's hands and sat down. "Hey there, David " the Mosquito said good-naturedly. "You mind your A's & P's and P's & Q's when you talk about my bag. It just so happens that I have a slight case of Acme under here and don't want to chance blemishing my reputation."

"Let's get serious," Litterbug said. "What's with the bag?"

"Why, I thought you knew, David. A famous insective like myself can't possibly give up his incognitohood just for the fame and fortune of late-night television. Now, if this were prime time . . . no. Not even then. It's essential that we top-of-the-line insectives keep our anonymousness—er, ah—anonymousity—um, ah, er—that the public doesn't know what we look like. We need to stay out of the public eye. If we don't keep a lid on our identity, we risk a serious lashing.

"As for the bag, that's just my generic, no-frills disguise. Like I always say, 'The pest stings in lice are flea.' And the bag is totally bio-degradable. Don't think people haven't tried to degrade me before.

"By the way, this is my deluxe bag. I'm two-faced, you know. This is the glad bag side. And then ... ugh ... if I turn it around ... urumph ... you can see my sad sack. There," Incognito said. Then he

struggled to pull his bag back into regulation position.

"Can I give you a hand there, Mosquito?" Litterbug offered. "I've got quite a few here. I'd never miss it."

"No. I can do it, thanks," the Mosquito replied. "It's just that success turns my head now and then and I sometimes have trouble getting it to face the right way again. Ah, here we go."

"You mentioned success, Mr. Mosquito. You've certainly had quite a lot of it. Tell us, how do you do what you do so well?"

"Well, David, I must say in all modesty that it comes out of my secret formula for success—99% desperation, 1% perspiration. A good deodor-ant helps too. Then there's simple self-control. I mean, if I don't control myself, who will? I have nerds of steel, you know."

From the look on his face, David Litterbug clearly did not have Incognito's nerds of steel. I.M. was beginning to get to him. It happened to everyone sooner or later.

"Moving right along, Mosquito," Litterbug said, "don't you get tired of all the traveling you have to do in the insective game? All those one-night stands? Living out of a suitcase?"

"Well, David, I don't always have to stand, you know. Some nights I actually get a bed. In a hotel, too—Ant Hil-tons or Roach Motels mostly. I hardly ever have

to live out of a suitcase anymore. But now and then I do get hive-sick, miss old fiends, that sort of thing." The Mosquito sighed.

"I suppose you'd call that the loneliness of the long-distance punner," Litterbug joked. "And now let's have a word from our sponsor. Ladies and germs, introducing the end to your cleaning problems—Licetoil. Let's hear a bit about it, shall we?"

As the commercial came on, Litterbug wiped his brow. "You know, Mr. Mosquito, I don't think I've ever wished for a

commercial interruption. Until now. Staying on track with you without losing my locomotion or getting run down is a real challenge."

"Why, thank you, Mr. L.," Incognito said just as they went on the air again.

Mr. Litterbug picked up the conversation with, "As we broke for the commercial, Incognito Mosquito was filling us in on the private life of a private insective. Tell us, Mr. Mosquito. Don't you get in some pretty life-threatening spots?"

"Oh sure, David. But there's always a way out. Like I'll never forget this one time. I was on a pirate ship and the bugganeers asked me to walk the plank. What did I do? I just bowed and said, 'After you.'"

"Did it work?" Litterbug asked in amazement.

"Well, actually, " the Mosquito replied, "it was a bit more complicated than that . . ."

1
The Case of the Unhinged Pirates

I was called in on the case by the navy's very own Admiral Hal F. Nelson. This bug was extremely well known in nautical circles. I couldn't fathom what he wanted me for. An in-depth insectigation?

Let's not go overboard here, Mosquito, I told myself. Don't get carried aweigh!

However, I had to admit it was quite an honor. Even for me. When they welcomed me on board, they gave me the official twenty-one-gun salute. That last one almost got me, too.

Admiral Nelson turned out to have more braids than Rebecca of Sunnybrook Farm. And he had enough purple hearts, orange stars, and yellow moons on his uniform to keep a medal detector busy for weeks.

Like the true military man that he was, the admiral wasted no time. "This case has baffled top military brains all over the country, Mosquito. So we decided to try reverse psychology—starting from the bottom up. That was how your name came up." The admiral made it clear that I was their last dope, so to speak. "Our case hinges on you now, Mosquito," he told me confidently.

Apparently a pirate ring was managing to smuggle gold out of our South Pacific port of Pago (formerly known as Pago Pago, but it's not half the place it used to be). But whenever the pirate ships were searched, no one could find a trace of the gold. Even the fillings in the pirates' teeth (what few they had) were silver. It was time to call in some outside mussel. That was where I came in.

"Don't worry, Admiral," I said reassuringly. "I'll pull the plug on this game, flush your smugglers out, and send them down the drain in no time."

So we weighed anchor (believe me, it was hea-vy!) and started out for Pago. Before I knew it, we were nearing our destination. I realized it was time for one of my world-famous disguises. I selected my John Les Feets pirate outfit. The costume comes complete with a supplementary appendage

package and a ten-galleon hat. It took me
only a minute to buckle my swashes. I was
soon off to meet Long John Silverfish,
suspected ringleader of the smuggling
operation, aboard his ship.

Walking along the Pago waterfront, I found the dock-side of the street really depressing. It was your basic squid roe, with sea urchins on every corner begging the lone sharks for a doubloon. Even a singloon.

The pirate ship turned out to be a real thug boat. I was a bit puzzled by her name—the S.S. *Thesaurus*—until I saw the traditional pirate flag, the "Jolly Roget."

Long John was not on board when I got there. And his crew was anything but aboveboard. Or above deck, for that matter. I found them below whooping it up. The guys were swilling ale and playing cards, paying off their bets with pieces of eight, nine, and even ten.

My aim was to try and loosen up the crowd. But boy, did they clam up on me. I went up to one old sea dog and just to make conversation asked if he had any fleas. I sure made anemone out of that one. Then I tried another approach. I swaggered up to a rather slimy first mate for a little inside info. "What's it all about, Algae?" I asked.

"Blimey! Before I gives you an answer to that one, me bucko, I wanna see some money change hands."

Always the agreeable one, I shrugged my shoulders and reached into my pocket for some bills. The pirate's greedy grin faded rapidly as I deftly passed the money from my left hand to my right.

Now the crowd turned ugly(er). Apparently I'd pushed these roughnecks too far. They looked ready to rough my neck up, not to mention knock my block off.

"All right, me hardy," the bugganeers said

to me, "we're gonna make you walk the plank." They led me to a board overhanging the rail and jabbed me in the back with a sharp instrument. I think it was a spoon. "Walk," they growled. So I did. Right to the end of the plank . . . and then right back to the ship on the underside. You see, I was wearing my gumshoes.

Fortunately, Long John Silverfish arrived at just that moment. He was truly the pirate's pirate. Even his tattoos had tattoos. He had a patch (natch) and a wooden leg to boot. Clearly this was a face that had launched a thousand gyps.

I introduced myself and before long had convinced Long John of my (in)sincerity. It was downhill from there. Before I knew it, I was accepted as one of the crew. We sealed our new partnership with a couple of gin yummies. "Bottoms up!" Long John cried. Strange custom, I thought to myself, as I nevertheless obligingly turned my full glass upside down.

Then Long John Silverfish proceeded to show me his entire operation. Aha! I thought. This is where I lower the boom. But was I ever in for a big surprise! Because there wasn't a sign of gold-smuggling. The only things that I could see being loaded onto the ship were small tin chests full of sea shells.

"We make quite a nice profit on the shells, mitey," Long John said. "Landlubbers luv 'em."

I was just about to remind him that my name was Les Feets, not Mitey, when a huge wind tipped the ship and almost blew me down.

"Better batten down yer patches, L.J.," I said, pointing to his eye (or lack thereof). "And don't forget yer wooden leg while you're at it. That wind kin sure shiver yer timbers."

I didn't have the chance to say anything

else. At that minute one of the chests that was being hoisted aboard flew open, showering me with shells. Then the wind blew the empty chest at me and it hit me on the head. Boy, did that chest pack a wallop! I was immediately knocked unconch-ious.

When I came to, the ship's sturgeon was giving me smelling sea salts. I felt like a real washout. Here I'd been on board a whole hour and I didn't have one clue to the gold. Even I, the great Incognito Mosquito, was beginning to flounder.

But I kept remembering Admiral Nelson's words: "Our case hinges on you, Mosquito." And I kept thinking about how heavy that supposedly empty tin chest was. Suddenly I realized that I had cracked another case. That is, if it hadn't cracked me first!

HOW DID INCOGNITO KNOW WHERE THE GOLD WAS?

Clearly Incognito Mosquito used his head to crack this caper wide open. He realized that since the only things being carried aboard were the chests full of sea shells, then the gold must somehow be hidden in the chests. But where?

It wasn't until one of the empty tin chests hit him that I.M. realized how heavy it was. He put that together with the admiral's offhand remark about the case hinging on him and . . . *voilà*. I.M. realized that the gold wasn't *in* the chests, the gold *was* the chests— the hinges, to be exact.

Long John Silverfish was sentenced to hard labor in an underwear factory. The ship's sturgeon was assigned to the prison pharmacy, where he is now known simply as the Bugman of Alka-Seltzer. The remainder of the crew were put to work in the prison dentist's office because, as Incognito Mosquito so aptly put it, "An aye, aye for a tooth, tooth."

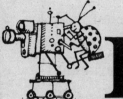

Incognito Mosquito seemed to know David's next guest from seeing just the top of his head. "Either that's a walking dust-broom or it's my old friend Mr. B from *The A-minus Team*!" he exclaimed as the studio audience burst into applause.

"Take that mosquito fool and teach him to breathe underwater!" responded Mr. B. "Hi, Mosquito, how you doin', man? Hi, David."

The big bee sat down, and Mr. Litterbug congratulated him on his starring role in the top-rated crimebusters TV series. Then he asked him about the negative response to the violence on the show. "Don't you get calls from mothers demanding that you strike the violence?"

But before Mr. B could reply, the Mosquito broke in. "Why all these complaints against violins? I mean, they're not my forte—I wouldn't want to string you along—but I don't see any reason to fret."

"We are discussing violence on TV, Mosquito. V-i-o-l-e-n-c-e," Mr. Litterbug injected pointedly, poking the Mosquito sharply.

"Ouch!" said Incognito Mosquito. "Sorry, David. It's hard to hear through this bag, you know. When they asked me if I wanted earholes, I thought they were offering earwigs so I said no thanks. Who needs hairy ears?"

"Could we just bag the comedy, Mosquito?" said Litterbug. "We're waiting to hear from Mr. B about *The A-minus Team* and TV violence."

I.M. nodded graciously. "Any sting you say, David."

"The team *is* trying to cool it on violence," said Mr. B. "We're into a new kind of slime fightin'. Like, before we destroy some fool's house, we dust for fingerprints. Then we destroy it. I bet you do the same thing, don't you, Mosquito?"

"Actually, no. I have a cleaning service that comes in once a week to dust for fingerprints. I myself am into electronic slime fighting."

"You mean you use a computer?" Litterbug asked. "No kidding! What kind? An IBM? An Apple? A Lemon?"

"Naturally I use a computer," I.M. said. "It's a special top-secret spy model available only to the FBI, the CIA, SWAT, and ME. It's called the Mata-Atari. A great little machine. I use it to keep track of crooks. Not to mention the ladybugs—I get their names from a date-a-bank."

"Speaking of banks, Mosquito," David Litterbug said, "didn't you solve a big bank case recently?"

"That's right," the Insective replied. "I don't want to brag but . . . in all immodesty I really knocked my client's socks off on that one. And that client had plenty of socks . . ."

2

Who Knows What the Nose Knows?

It was a dark and swarmy night. I was awakened from a deep sleep by a call from one of my co–crime fighters, my old friend Thomas Maggot, P.I. You may know him as that famous TV insectigator from

Hawaii. He's so clean-cut that one of these days I expect to see him doing guest spots on the soaps, like *The Young and the Nestless* or *The Days of Our Hives*.

Maggot was really in a lather. "Mosquito," my old pal began, "I'm the strong, silent type. A man of few words. So I'll give it to you straight. HELP! Come quick."

The place I came to was the scene of the slime—the First Gnational Bank and Mistrust Company. It had recently merged with Manufacturers Handover to become a full-fledged savings and loan offering tix shelters and money markets, if you can buy that.

Maggot needed my help on an emergency case. (Even if a case isn't an emergency to start with, it is when I get there.) This one was an emergency of the first magnumitude. The usually cool Maggot was wound up like a time bomb ready to go off—tick, tick, tick.

"Hey, relax, Maggot," I said. "Don't go to pieces on me."

"Sorry, I.M.," Maggot apologized. "I guess I'm used to life as a Hawaii-flii, where I lei back and take it easy. I think I'm starting to crack under the pressure. They're really making me scramble on this one."

"It's okay. Why don't you just give me the case in an eggshell?" I replied reassuringly. Maggot is basically a good egg. A little cracked. But good.

"Well, okay. If that's how you want it," Thomas said doubtingly. "Here's how it goes. The president of the bank, a Mr. C. Note,

37

was assaulted as he was closing the vault at the end of the day, and the vault was bugglarized. The alarm system tipped off the security team. But by the time they arrived, over a million dollars in stocks, bonds, and variable-rate insecurities had been taken. There was nothing they could do but call an ambulance and me. There was nothing I could do but call you.

"We have absolutely no clues, no fingerprints, no nothing. The only other person we found at the scene of the crime was a teller, a Mr. Mort Gage," Maggot said, pointing to a figure huddled in the corner. "He was out cold but unhurt when we arrived."

Maggot and I moved over to question what seemed to be our only lead. Fortunately, the man pulled himself together and was able to tell us his story.

"I-I-I think I may have the information

you're looking for," he said. "I realize it's
my d-d-duty as an upstanding citizen to talk.
I saw the whole thing. I worked late today.
I was j-j-just about to leave when I saw a
bug with a stocking over his head punch
my boss in the face and knock him out. I
was surprised it took only one punch to
knock him out. My boss rules the bank with
an iron hand, but I guess he must have a
glass jaw. Unless . . . oh, my! Unless the boss
was just pretending. Unless the boss was
really in on it. Oh! I'd be shattered. Any-

way," the teller continued, "I was so scared myself that I fainted there on the spot. Oh d-d-dear! I'm so ashamed."

After comforting the teller, Maggot and I left him collapsed on the couch. "Sofa, so good," I said. "I think our next stop is the

hospital. Maybe we can get a better description of this stocking bugglar from C. Note."

We immediately headed over to Our Lady of Perpetual Motion Hospital. Sure enough, it was. The place was buzzing frantically with nurses, doctors, orderlies, and dis-orderlies when we arrived. Even Dr. Dolittle was busy.

We were pointed toward Mr. C. Note's physician. I went up and shook his hand. "Dr. Livingsting, I presume?"

"No," he replied.

"No?" I asked.

"Yes," he replied.

By this point I was naturally thoroughly confused. Even more than usual. And I was growing in-patient besides. "So which is it, fella?" I said. "Are you Dr. No or are you just another Yes man?"

"Yes, the name is Dr. No, sir. And no, sir, I'm not a Yes man. The doctor you're looking for is over there." He sent me off with a friendly shot in the arm.

Without further ado Maggot and I made our way to Dr. Livingsting. "So, what's up, Doc?" I asked. He assured us that it was all right to question the patient briefly. "But I must warn you, Mr. Note is feeling pretty grouchy."

"That bad, huh?" I said sympathetically. "Well, Thomas, I guess that means we'll have to look for our Mr. C. Note in the Offensive Care Unit."

When we entered the room, we found that we could have questioned Mr. Note until we were blue in the face. It wouldn't have made any difference, because *he* was so black and blue in the face that he couldn't

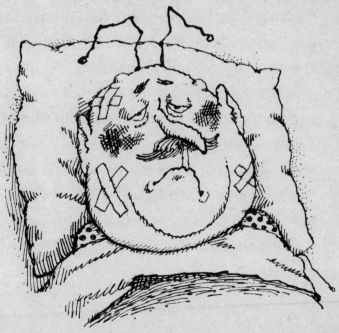

say a word. Basically all Mr. C. Note could do was grunt. Both of his cheeks were so swollen that you could hardly make out his nose. In fact, his nose was the only part of his face still in reasonably good condition after the brutal attack. All in all, it was a pretty good nose, as far as noses run.

Maggot was stunned. "Wow! I didn't think the poor guy would be in such bad shape after just one punch."

"Well, no bruise is good bruise, you know, Thomas," I said. "And that goes double for this one. Because we've been double-crossed—by the teller, that is!"

Maggot nearly fell through the floor. It just goes to show you, I thought to myself. Brains, brawn, and a pretty face aren't everything. I'm not sure what's left. But I was sure of one thing. That teller wasn't telling all.

Thomas recovered quickly. "Mosquito,

I've got to hand it to you. When you've got it, you've got it. Whatever it is. I just hope it isn't catching. Now, tell me. How did you know the teller did it?"

WHY DID INCOGNITO SUSPECT THE TELLER?

Incognito realized that if Mr. C. Note had been hit only once, as the teller claimed, both of his cheeks couldn't possibly be bruised unless his nose was smashed too. But Mr. Note's nose turned out to be the only thing left intact.

Therefore I.M. concluded that the teller had pulled the job himself. He knocked out the bank president, hid the loot in his desk,

1.

and then pretended to faint to escape suspicion. He then said Mr. C. Note had gone down with only one punch to shed suspicion on *him*—to blacken his reputation as well as his eyes.

Later on, after all the attention died down, the teller planned to simply sneak the money out and live happily ever after. But he hadn't counted on Incognito Mosquito, Private Insective. The teller lost by a nose.

The crooked teller drew a life sentence—compounded quarterly.

Mr. B and David Litterbug were both amazed by Incognito Mosquito's genius. They were struck. Positively speechless. It took the Mosquito a minute to realize that he had, in fact, accidentally hit both men in the mouth in his effort to reenact the case. And true to form, each formed only a single bruise.

I.M., on the other hand, formed two big dents—one on each side of his paper bag. "Maybe I should have turned the other cheek," he said, smiling sickly. "I always was a little starstruck."

Litterbug tactfully chose that moment to

announce his next guest. "I take great pleasure in introducing a bug who worked his way through electoral college, was valeticktorian of his class, and may now be on his way to the guber-gnatorial seat. Let's welcome His Honor Mayor Ed Kochroach."

The mayor had just penned a best seller, *High-Flying Mayor,* and David started off by asking why he'd picked that title.

"Because I try harder and fly higher," said the mayor. "Also, some people think I have an inflated opinion of myself. I've even been told that I'm full of hot air! But I think that's blowing things out of proportion."

"Can you tell us a little about your book, Mr. Mayor?"

"Why, sure, David. I can even tell you a lot about it," answered Mayor Kochroach. "What I wanted to do was to let bugs everywhere know what it's like to be infested with the power of running America's largest city. So in my book I really get down to the city nitty-gritty. And that's as it should be. I really smell it like it is.

"In that respect, my job and that of Mr.

Mosquito here are alike. Incidentally, Mosquito, I'm really impressed with the job you're doing. Why, if this country didn't have top slime fighters like yourself who go around discovering injustice, we might never know it's there. How do you do it? And by the way, how'm I doing?"

I.M. answered, "Mr. Mayor, you're doing great. As for your other question, you can always find crime when you want it. All you have to do is look. For a start, crime begins in the home.

"Take the time I met this cute little lightning bug. Boy, did she turn me on! So I invited her up to the hive to see my itchings. I'm on the Ten Best Nest List, you know. Little did I know that she was a paid killer. One of my many enemies had put out a contract on me. Only I hadn't agreed to the terms. She pulled out a pistol and said, 'Sorry about that, Mosquito. The

bug stops here.' Fortunately for me, she was a rotten shot. But it just goes to show you can't be too careful. The next day I went out and got a bullet-proof nest.

"Anyway, as I was saying before I so rudely interrupted myself, you can find crime almost anywhere. Why, there's even crime under jackets, between leaves, and on spines."

"Where?" asked the mayor.

I.M. smiled confidently. "In books, naturally. Books have spines, leaves, and jackets. Would you believe it, there's even crime in the library? Yes, I remember . . ."

3

Who's Most Liable to Steal a Bible?

I remember it all so well. The call came on a Friday. I was searching for my glasses at the time. I was in the middle of *Robinson Crusoe* and I simply couldn't see Friday without them. I actually have three

pairs of glasses—one for nearsightedness, one for farsightedness, and one for locating the other two pairs. I don't usually wear any, though. They make me stand out. And I'm outstanding enough. I really don't like to make a spectacle of myself.

In this case, however, reading glasses seemed appropriate. You see, the call came from the public library. I have a binding contract with them. Whenever they have a problem, they just page me.

It seems someone had stolen the priceless

Gutenbug Bible on loan to the library. Apparently the thief had not been aware of the library's elaborate security system. Alarms sounded, buzzers alerted the police, and the entire library was automatically sealed off. The criminal had disappeared into the stacks with the Bible, unable to escape.

When I arrived, the library doors were still locked and its occupants were in a noisy

panic. What a ruckus! It was obvious that this library utilized the famed Dewey Decibel system.

I had just begun looking over the crowd, trying to figure out who was a lowly enough bookworm to steal the Bible, when a police officer came to tell me I had been summoned by "the highest authority."

"The highest authority!" I gulped. "I know it's a Bible and everything, but don't you think we're getting a little carried away here?"

Fortunately, "the highest authority" was none other than the library's director, one Dr. Rita Book. She turned out to be an avid mystery reader and a charter member of the Agatha Chrysalis Fan Club. Which naturally bowled me over. This woman was right up my alley. I just hoped I could score on this case without striking out.

"I'd like to fill you in on what happened, Mr. Mosquito," Dr. Book said, crossing her

legs. And legs. And legs. "This is the first robbery we've ever had here. The Guten-bug Bible is a historical treasure, you know. It's the first book ever printed on a printing press. Before that, all books were copied by

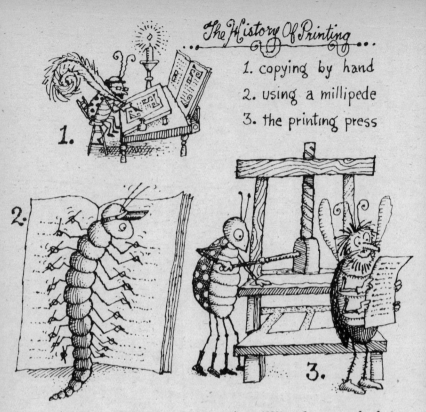

1. copying by hand
2. using a millipede
3. the printing press

hand. Of course, using a millipede speeded things up, but the printing press was a huge jump.

"This Bible's on loan from the Soviet Onion's Ministry of Finants," explained Dr. Book. "They're planning to auction it at Sothebee's and raise a bundle. We'll be in big trouble if we let the world's most valuable book get stolen right from under our noses. In other words, this whole thing really stinks and I want us to come out smelling like a rose. That's why we're in such a russia to find it. Kapish?"

I could see Dr. Book was beginning to get antsy—wringing her hands and hands and hands. "So-viet, Dr. Book," I said. "Lettuce not worry. The Soviet Onion will never know about the missing Bible. I'm sure it will turn-ip before you know it. They don't call me the Cellery Queen of the insect world for nothing."

I first considered consulting the Bible-iography. Nah, I thought to myself. Too easy. Even for me.

So I turned instead to checking out the bugs in the library. First I ran into a woman in the astronomy section. When I asked her about the theft she answered simply, "No comet."

Searching through the stacks, I spotted several of my favorite books. I remember I used to read J.R.R. Tolkien for hours on end. It was downright hobbit-forming. Then, of course, my favorite classics—*Withering Flights, The Three Louseketeers,* and *The Great Gadfly* by that famous photographer turned novelist, F. Stop Fitzgerald.

Next I came across a studious young bug whose eyes were so crossed that he could read two pages of a book at once—the left page with his right eye and the right page

with his left. Unfortunately, he hadn't seen anything suspicious out of either eye.

My next stop was a woman frantically flipping through the cookbooks. "So what's cooking?" I asked. But she only sizzled at me. I think she had just two minutes to find a recipe for a three-minute egg. Clearly she was going stir crazy. When I asked whether she knew anything about the theft, I thought she was going to boil over. "No need to get in a stew," I said. I could see she was too hot to handle, so I quickly desserted her.

Finally I came to an elderly librarian who was shelving books. She was so hunched over that she could barely move. I believe the term is quasi-motile. She also turned out to be half deaf, as I found out when I said hello. Again. And again. The librarian was muttering something under her breath. She was annoyed when I introduced myself and interrupted her work.

"Sherlock. Go holmes!" she said, throwing a heavy volume at me.

"Ah," I remarked while picking it up, "a flying Chaucer."

"Can't you see I'm trying to shelve my books?" she squawked at me. "You youngsters have no respect for the classics. Look at what someone did. They put *Twenty Thousand Legs Under the Flea* up here on the top shelf, and *Charlotte's Web* right here next to the bottom. Don't they teach you the alphabet anymore?"

Up until that point I'd been listening to the old librarian sympathetically. But all of a sudden I knew it was time to do my duty. I had to book her for the theft of the Gutenbug Bible.

HOW DID INCOGNITO KNOW THE LIBRARIAN WAS THE THIEF?

Every librarian knows that storybooks are shelved according to authors' last names—not titles. Therefore, *Twenty Thousand Legs Under the Flea* by Jules Verne should be shelved before *Charlotte's Web* by E. Bee White.

The so-called librarian turned out to be none other than Sleazy Louisey, the light-fingered louse. She was sentenced to do *Hard Times* in the prison arc-hives.

The Bible was just where Sleazy Louisey said she'd hidden it. Ironically, she'd put it in a dark corner of the mystery section known as the Alfred Nitchcock.

After a brief commercial message, the mayor and Mr. B excused themselves and David brought on his next two guests. They turned out to be none other than the famous tennis stars Bjorn Bug and John McEnroach.

The bugs had just started to chat about the game when Incognito commented on what a good-natured sport tennis is.

"After all," he said, "where else does the loser still report his score as love? And where else do the players have such a good time netting all that money? What a racket! And to top it off, they all have a ball!"

"Gimme a break," said Mr. McEnroach.
"Tennis may be good. But it's not that good.
We're talkin' a tough sport for tough guys.
And don't you forget it, Mosquito."

"Yah," added Mr. Bug.

"Believe me, I can see what's what," continued McEnroach. "Just like I can always see whether the ball is in or out. But the judges never accept my call. I've had to throw so many fits on the court that some bugs think I'd be better off as a major-league pitcher."

"Yah," added Mr. Bug.

"Still, wouldn't you say—" began I.M.

"Do you think doing all those Tic disposable razor commercials is a picnic?" interrupted McEnroach. "Sometimes just getting through the rehearsals in one piece is a close shave. Come on. Gimme a break. If you don't, I'm gonna walk right off this stage. I'm warning you . . ."

"Yah," added Mr. Bug.

"Quick, Mosquito," David injected. "Give him a break. Give him a break."

"You know, Mr. McEnroach," Incognito ejected, "I have the utmost respect for you pro tennis players. But I do have this gut feeling that you're painting a rather dismal picture here. I mean, it's not as though you have to work without a net or anything. And with the money you and players like Martina Navratilarva make, you can Chase Manhattan Bank around the tennis circuit. Admit it. Aren't you being just a bit high-strung about this whole thing?"

"Gimme a break, Mosquito. Let's face it. Tennis is a tough call all the way down the line. The game is no party," Mc-Enroach concluded.

"You may have a point there, Big Mac," I.M. said. "But you know, the private insective game is no party either. That is, except for this one time . . ."

4

The Louisiana Fur-Chase

 was just about to jump into my new Italian sportscar—a Bugatti with all the trimmings. Even the windshield wipers had wipers. I had planned to catch a baseball game that afternoon— an inning on my outing, so to speak.

Then out of the blue I was hit in the face by a UFP—an unidentified flying package. "What a pain!" I exclaimed, studying the invader. "Just as I suspected. Parcel Pest. Must be important."

I carefully unwrapped the box and took off the lid, exposing its contents. Immediately my defective reasoning powers were at work. It was a mask of some kind. "Ah, what a handsome devil!" I exclaimed. "Looks vaguely familiar, too. Could it be the face of some dashing television star? A famous political figure? A Greek god?"

I tried the mask on while looking in the mirror. It fit perfectly. I just couldn't take my eyes off myself. I would have carried on my "menage a mois" indefinitely, but I spotted a note in the box out of the corner of my eye. You need a square head to be able to do that, you know.

The note read:

Dear Mr. Mosquito,

I'all would be mitey honored if y'all would be my all's security honor guard at this year's mardi grass and Masquerade Ball.

I can promise you a rip-roarin' good time.

Evil Bollregard Weevil

The invitation was most inviting. I'd always wanted to meet that re-tired motorcycle daredevil. So I packed a bag and by the next afternoon was at Weevil's Louisiana plantation outside New Orleans. I would have been there earlier except that I wanted to see the sun shine bright on my old Kentucky home and to take a minute to tie a yellow ribbon round the old oak tree.

Mr. Weevil couldn't have been more
hospitable. He even had the plantation
serv-ants on 24-hour duty to wait on guests
at any hour. Basically, you see, the Mardi
Grass is a 24-hour-a-day week-long party.
At Mr. Weevil's invitation, bugs had flown
in from all over the country for the festiv-
ities. "I cotton to you yankee doodle bugs"
is the way Mr. Weevil put it.

It was clear to my keen insective brain, however, that this trip was not going to be all fun and games. No indeed. There was more here than met the fly. It was not long before Mr. Weevil took me aside.

"Y'all see that city slicker over yonder?" Weevil asked in a hushed whisper. "That is none other than the notorious fur thief, Mr. Simon LeFlea. I declare I'm more'n a bit nervous 'bout him—seein's how I got one of the biggest dang fur collections in the whole cotton-pickin' country. Why, I got so many furs that I need to remind myself every now and again to 'leave it to beaver.'"

"If I might be so bold, Mr. Weevil, can you tell me why you even invited LeFlea if you feared for your furs?"

"Well, that there's the tricky part, son. It looks like LeFlea has gone and swept my daughter off her feet. All of 'em! See? Look yonder at that porch."

Sho'nuff. I looked at the veranda and saw LeFlea romancing Belle Weevil. I could see why Mr. Weevil was so worried. Belle was a petite, defenseless little thing—definitely the lesser of two weevils.

"Don't you worry, Mr. Weevil," I said. "I'll keep an eye on them both." And I did, too. Which was not so easy. Because there were parties all over New Orleans.

A few nights later we all went off to the fancy Mardi Grass Masquerade Ball. That's when I got to wear that handsome mask that looked so much like me. Boy, what a lawn party that costume ball was! It really mowed me down.

Naturally, some seedy characters managed to find their way in. It was almost impossible to weed out the bad guise from the good guise. And it wasn't long before some of them got kind of rowdy. There was one bug dressed in a furry monster suit who

kept falling into the fountain. But it turned out to be okay, since the outfit was wash-and-werewolf.

I had a delightful chat with a group of bugs dressed as the most famous singing group of all time—the Beetles. John, Paul,

George, and Ringworm were discussing the hatching of a new Monarch butterfly in Buggingham Palace. Unfortunately, I had to cut our talk short. Duty called. "Coming, duty," I answered.

"Cheerio!" the Beetles said cheerfully.

"Rice krispy," I responded snappily.

And there were other distractions. I met a gorgeous young vermine all wrapped in ermine. We danced to the music of the Harmony Grits. Unfortunately, the conductor kept having tempo tantrums. One minuet we were dancing, the next we weren't. I was practically climbing the waltz.

So I just stopped and looked at my partner. And if you think she looked great, you

should have gotten a whiff of her. Heaven scent! We set up a date for the next night— "same time, same Chanel."

Although I saw Belle Weevil on and off during the evening—naturally she was the belle of the ball—I didn't see Simon LeFlea at all. But I must admit that I didn't think much of it at the time. You see, there were other things to think about.

For instance, the food. The waiters kept passing tray after tray. I was sorely tempted to sample some of those luscious sugar-nut southern sweets, but I was painfully famil- iar with the perils of praulines. The last time I ate some I had to pay my dentist on the installment plan. He had to install a separate chair just for me.

The drinks didn't make my work any easier either. By mid-ball I'd had one too many Dixie cups of cotton gin and tonic and was developing a rapidly blossoming case of Southern Discomfort. So I left the ballroom and hightailed it back to the Weevil plantation. When I got there shortly after midnight, the scene was sobering. Mr. Weevil's prize fur collection had been stolen!

I could see that it was time for me to step in. I turned to Mr. Weevil, who, needless to say, was not looking too thrilled with me.

"Tell me, Mr. Weevil," I began, "when did you first notice that the fur collection was missing?"

"Mosquito," he said through gritted teeth, "you may recall that I invited you down here to keep an eye on the situation. A private eye. Unfortunately, up till now you've been so private that no one's been able to find you. I'm awful glad you finally found us. But I'd rather you'd missed us. In fact, the best thing about you is your absence. That seems to be the only kind of sense you've got. Speakin' of absence, everybody

is accounted for except for Mr. LeFlea. Now, that's strange. Although not unexpected.

"For your information," Weevil continued, "I just found out the furs were gone. With the Mardi Grass on an' all, and with so many folks comin' an' goin', I hadn't personally checked on the furs since the day before yesterday. So they could've been taken anytime within the last few days—or make that the last few daze in your case."

"Gee, Mr. Weevil, no need to get insulting," I said. "If this is the way you treat your crooks, you don't deserve to have any."

My next step was to ask for witnesses. Finally an older man came forward and identified himself as Pollin, the relief butler. He was so old that it was a relief if he didn't have to go on duty.

"Pardon me, sir," he creaked. "Perhaps I can help. I looked out the window of my quarters earlier and I believe I saw someone lurking around the fur vault at approximately eleven o'clock. I really didn't give it a thought, sir. That is, until I heard about the robbery. Frightfully sorry, sir."

"Tell me, Pollin," I asked, "could you identify this not-so-innocent flystander?"

Mr. Weevil stepped forward. "Oh, that wouldn't be likely, Mr. Mosquito. You see, the sun shines directly into Pollin's window at that time of the mornin', and I'm afraid old Pollin's eyes are pretty sensitive. I don't reckon he could've seen a thing."

"Uh-hum," I said thoughtfully. But I was still in the dark. It was going to take a bit longer for me to see things clearly.

Then suddenly the light hit me—*ouch!*— and I knew I knew. I raised my hand and pointed a finger at . . .

WHO DID INCOGNITO MOSQUITO FINGER AS THE FUR THIEF?

The fur thief was none other than Mr. Bollregard Weevil himself. I.M. realized that Pollin never specified whether he'd spotted the suspect near the fur vault at 11 A.M. or 11 P.M. Since the serv-ants were on 24-hour duty, it could have been either.

Most bugs would have assumed that the theft occurred at night. Unless they knew otherwise—from first-under-handed experience. By talking about the sun shining in Pollin's eyes, Mr. Weevil proved that he

knew the bugglary happened in broad day-light. The bug Pollin saw from his window was in fact one of the thugs that Mr. Weevil had hired to pull off the fake robbery.

Mr. Weevil confessed that he'd hoped to frame LeFlea in order to keep the notorious bug from marrying his daughter. Unfortunately for him, the plan backfired. Instead of putting LeFlea on ice, Weevil got the cold shoulder from Belle. But at least the furs went back in cold storage.

David Litterbug's next two guests were those dashing sci-fly film-makers, Steven Spielbug and George Locust. Incognito was excited. *Star Worms*, *Indiana Jones and the Pimple of Doom*, and *Raiders of the Lost Ant* were some of his favorite movies. I.M. asked what the famed shutterbugs planned to do next.

Locust answered, "We're thinking of moving to a new studio. Up to now we've been with Paramoth and Twentieth Centipede-Fox. But we really want the chance to work with that old screen gem, Cecil B. DeMillipede. It would be a whole new leg in our career."

"I hope that doesn't mean that Luke Flyswatter has swatted his last fly, Mr. Locust. And isn't it kind of unfair to change studios?" Incognito questioned. "I mean, like switching horseflies in midstream. Biting the hive that feeds you, you might say."

"No, Mosquito, *you* might say," Spielbug corrected sharply. "Our intentions are purely honorable. We just want the chance to try something new. We've already decided that our next film is going to be about tissue transplants, but we still need some time to organ-ize our operation."

It looked as if I.M. had rubbed the two science friction authorities the wrong way. At that moment Locust whispered into David Litterbug's ear.

"Gee, fellas," Litterbug replied. "That's most unusual. But . . . ah . . . if, um . . . Well, why don't you ask him yourselves?"

Locust and Spielbug smiled. "We have a surprise for you, Mr. Mosquito. When we found out you were going to be on the show tonight, we hatched a little plot. We made up a mystery story of our own, and we want to see if you can find the bugs in it. Unless of course you don't want to put yourself to the test . . ."

"No, no. Don't be such pestimists. I rise to the challenge. It keeps me on my toes. You bet your lice I'll give it a try. So fire away, gentlemen."

Here is the strange story that George Locust and Steven Spielbug told:

5

The Brief Case of the Unlawful Lawyer

The famous lawyer Lee Gull had just gotten home, hung up his legal suit, and jumped into bed. However, he was having a lot of trouble falling asleep. He'd spent the entire day in court on a very trying

95

case. His client, Mr. Meana, was charged with humicide. The persecution claimed that Mr. Meana had hanged his friend. Mr. Gull was looking for a suspended sentence on the grounds that the other side didn't have a leg to stand on.

All of a sudden Mr. Gull heard the sound of breaking glass downstairs. He jumped out of bed and grabbed his old navy sword, which was emblazoned with his colonel's stripes.

"I got this sword from General Patton Leather. 'Old Spit 'n Polish' we used to call him. And I'm not over the anthill yet!" he thought to himself as he charged down the stairs to nab the intruders. Unfortunately, he arrived just as the crooks were rushing out the front door.

"Curses," Gull said as he stuck the sword in his loophole. "Foiled again! And I would so have sabered catching those bandits."

After calling the police, Lee Gull grabbed an illegal pad and pencil and went to see what had been taken. A quick inventory showed that all the silver was gone. Also, a few objects d'art were missing. Mr. Gull didn't mind about them so much, since he had objected to them when his wife bought them in the first place.

And besides, everything was covered by a generous blanket insurance policy. In fact, the Gulls didn't just own a piece of the rock, they lived under it.

However, Mr. Gull was very upset to find glass all over his flower beds. His prize blossoms were ruined. Apparently the thieves had jumped over the fence and broken in through the downstairs window.

"I'll get you crooks," he said angrily. "I'll give each one of you the fattest tu-lips you've ever seen. I'll squeeze the breath zinnia out of you! When I'm through with you, you'll be gladiola to go to jail. I didn't spend four years in law school for nothing!"

But no crooks were caught, and when Mr. Gull tried to claim the insurance, Judge J. Risdiction threw his case out of court for three reasons. Mite-igating circumstances, you mite say.

WHAT WERE THE THREE BUGS IN LEE GULL'S STORY?

Incognito Mosquito had no trouble spotting the three bugs in the story.

First, there are no colonels in the navy. (Neither are there any generals.) Lee Gull had never been near the navy, and his sword was a fake.

Second, law school lasts only three years, not four. So Lee Gull wasn't even a bona fide lawyer.

Third, if the thieves had broken *into* Mr. Gull's house through the window, as he claimed, the broken glass would have been *inside* the room, not outside in the flower garden.

Lee Gull's whole story was nothing but a scam to defraud the insurance company.

Everyone was amazed at how Incognito Mosquito managed to solve this illegal puzzle. Spielbug and Locust accepted their defeat gracefully with a token "Bar, humbug."

Litterbug then stepped in with, "Mosquito, will you do me one favor? Anyone who is as good as you are at what you do should have no fear of revealing his identity. So would you please take off your bag?"

With surprising grace, I.M. agreed. "I've always considered myself a top undercover agent. But maybe you're right. The time has come to bag this bag."

He removed the sack . . . only to reveal another bag underneath. The audience broke into spontaneous applause (there's no accounting for audiences).

It was clear that the show was drawing to a close. In David's words, "What more could possibly happen?

"And by the way," Litterbug continued, "let me tell you about tomorrow's guests, although I must admit that Incognito Mosquito, Private Insective, is a hard act to follow. Tomorrow night we'll be expecting frontier chef Betty Crockett and that famous football he-roach Joe Na-moth. We'll also meet Tick Jagger, lead singer of the Rolling Drones. Till then, good night, everybody."

As Incognito Mosquito exited the stage door, he was mobbed by bugs wanting his autograph. He greeted his fans warmly with that mysterious I.M. smile. Then, taking the autograph books one by one, he wrote:

Roses are red,
So's a caboose.
I'm incognito.
What's your excuse?
Wormest regards,
X

Why the X, you might ask? Because if he signed his name, he wouldn't be incognito, would he?

About the Author

E. A. Hass shares a New York City apartment with two lazy, literate cats. In the summer there are usually several dozen mosquitoes around as well, any one of which could be *the* mosquito.

E. A. buzzes around doing all kinds of things, many of which involve two favorite subjects—children and books. In addition to being an author and publicist, Hass appears as Dr. Book on American Public Radio's *Kids America* show, diagnosing book ailments and dispensing prescriptions for good reading. Example: "Read two chapters of Incognito Mosquito and call me in the morning."

About the Artist

Don Madden lives with his wife, son, and daughter in an old farmhouse in upstate New York. They share the place with a large scraggly dog and a small flabby cat, who spend their time trading fleas. Before moving to the country Mr. Madden studied and taught at the Philadelphia Museum College of Art. Now he illustrates children's books and fights off hordes of six-legged visitors.